Northamptonshire
County Council
Libraries and Information Ser

D0539470

RYAN, M.

New kit on the block

Please return or renew this item by the last date shown.
You may renew items (unless they have been requested
by another customer) by telephoning, writing to or calling
in at any library. ♻ 100% recycled paper BKS \\ (5/95)

DISCARDED
Northamptonshire Libraries

80 001 861 290

Sch

Fat Alphie and Charlie the Wimp

Make friends with the greatest alley cats in town!

Be sure to read:

The Disappearing Dinner
Fat Alphie in Love

... and lots, lots more!

New Kit on the Block

Margaret Ryan
illustrated by Jacqueline East

SCHOLASTIC

For Zoë, with love – M.R.

Northamptonshire Libraries & Information Service	
Peters	05-Sep-02
CF	£3.99

Scholastic Children's Books,
Commonwealth House, 1-19 New Oxford Street,
London, WC1A 1NU, UK
a division of Scholastic Ltd
London ~ New York ~ Toronto ~ Sydney ~ Auckland
Mexico City ~ New Delhi ~ Hong Kong

First published by Scholastic Ltd, 2002

Text copyright © Margaret Ryan, 2002
Illustrations copyright © Jacqueline East, 2002

ISBN 0 439 98104 2

All rights reserved

Printed and bound by Oriental Press, Dubai, UAE

10 9 8 7 6 5 4 3 2 1

The rights of Margaret Ryan and Jacqueline East to be identified as the author and illustrator of this work respectively have been asserted by them in accordance with the Copyright, Designs and Patents Act, 1988.

This book is sold subject to the condition that it shall not, by way of trade or otherwise, be lent, resold, hired out, or otherwise circulated without the publisher's prior consent in any form of binding or cover other than that in which it is published and without a similar condition, including this condition, being imposed upon the subsequent purchaser.

 Chapter One

All was peaceful at number three Wheelie
Bin Avenue. Fat Alphie licked the last of the
cream bun from his whiskers and settled
down in the big armchair for a quiet
snooze. Charlie the Wimp padded round
about him.

"Go to sleep, Charlie," yawned Fat Alphie. "In a minute," muttered Charlie the Wimp. "I like to sleep with my rubber duck, but I can't find it anywhere."

Charlie searched under
the bramble bush,
but his rubber
duck wasn't
there.

He searched
under the garden
gnome, but it
wasn't there either.

He even searched
under Fat Alphie's
tail, but there
was no sign of
his rubber duck.

Fat Alphie flicked his tail and sighed. "Go to sleep, Charlie," he yawned.

"In a minute," muttered Charlie the Wimp. "I like to sleep with my jingly ball, but I can't find that anywhere either."

Charlie searched under
the gooseberry bush,
but his jingly ball
wasn't there.

He searched under
the bird bath, but it
wasn't there either.

He even rolled
Fat Alphie over
and searched
under him, but
there was no sign
of his jingly ball.

Fat Alphie rolled back and sighed.

"Never mind your rubber duck or your jingly ball, Charlie," he said. "Lie down, close your eyes and I'll tell you a story."

"Oh good," said Charlie. "I love a story. Tell me the one about the two cats who were very best friends."

"Okay," said Fat Alphie. "Once upon a time there were two cats called Fat Alphie and Charlie the Wimp…"

ZZZZZZZZ… Charlie was asleep.

ZZZZZZZZ… So was Fat Alphie.

Fat Alphie dreamed of lots of cream buns,
and snored and flicked his ears.

Charlie the Wimp dreamed of lots of
silvery fish, and snuffled and flicked his tail.

Suddenly...

JINGLY JINGLY,
QUACK QUACK.
JINGLY JINGLY,
QUACK QUACK.

Charlie the Wimp woke with a start.

"What was that?" Tied to his tail with some wool were his rubber duck and his jingly ball.

"Who did that!" yelled Charlie. He chased his tail round and round trying to get them off, till he was dizzy and had to sit down.

"Hey, good joke, good joke," piped a squeaky voice.

"It's not funny at all," muttered Charlie. He looked round and saw a tiny kitten trampolining on Fat Alphie's tummy.

Fat Alphie woke up
on an extra high
bounce.

"Who's that?"
he cried.

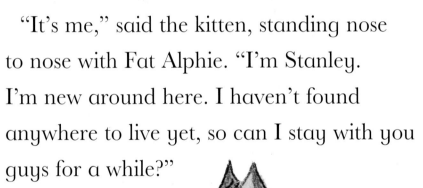

"It's me," said the kitten, standing nose
to nose with Fat Alphie. "I'm Stanley.
I'm new around here. I haven't found
anywhere to live yet, so can I stay with you
guys for a while?"

"No," said Charlie the Wimp, clutching his rubber duck and his jingly ball. "We don't like having our toys tied to our tails. Go away!"

"Wait a minute, Charlie," said Fat Alphie. "This little fellow's kind of cute. I think we should let him stay. After all, what harm can a little kitten do?"

Chapter Two

Stanley grinned.

"Thanks," he said. "I'll just get my things."

He dived under the hedge and dragged out a large bag, and spread out his belongings. There were squeaky mice, bits of string and half-chewed slippers everywhere.

"Look at the mess he's making," cried Charlie the Wimp, "and I've just tidied up."

"He's just a kitten," laughed Fat Alphie. "Stop moaning, Charlie. I bet you were messy at his age too."

"Wasn't," muttered Charlie.

"And here are all my friends," said
Stanley, as lots of kittens appeared and
jumped all over Charlie.

"Help, get them off me," yelled Charlie
the Wimp.

Fat Alphie laughed. "They're just kittens. Stop moaning, Charlie."

"Yes, stop moaning, Charlie," giggled Stanley as he and his friends played tug of war with Charlie's whiskers,

nibbled Charlie's tail,

and shouted BOO in Charlie's ear.

Charlie stopped moaning. He climbed up on to the wheelie bin and stayed there.

Later that day, Millie the Mouser, One-eared Tom and Clever Claws strolled past.

"What are you doing up there, Charlie?" asked Millie the Mouser.

"Nothing," muttered Charlie.

"Are you in a huff, Charlie?" asked One-eared Tom.

"No," muttered Charlie.

"I don't think he likes these kittens trying to catch his tail," said Clever Claws.

"They're only playing," laughed Fat
Alphie. "Just look at Stanley bouncing on
my tummy!"

BOING! BOING! BOING!

"You can come down now, Charlie," called Fat Alphie a little while later. "Stanley and his friends have gone and it's nearly time to go out for dinner."

Charlie looked around nervously. It seemed to be safe so he slid down from the bin.

"I don't know why you had to go up there in the first place," said Fat Alphie. "Stanley's such a nice young kitten. We had great fun this afternoon."

Charlie said nothing.

They strolled down to Sid's Diner for
Fat Alphie's tuna-fish starter.

Sid was just putting out some rubbish.

"Oh, there you are, Fat Alphie," he said.
"I didn't expect to see you. Your young
friend, Stanley, said you wouldn't be
coming tonight, so I gave him your tuna-
fish starter instead. Sorry."

"That's okay," said Fat Alphie. "He must have made a mistake."

Charlie the Wimp said nothing.

They walked down to McPheeline's, the butcher's, for Fat Alphie's steak.

Mr McPheeline was just pulling down the blinds.

"Oh, there you are, Fat Alphie," he said. "I didn't expect to see you. Your young friend, Stanley, said you wouldn't be coming tonight, so I gave him the steak for your main course instead. Sorry."

"That's strange," frowned Fat Alphie. "Surely he can't have made another mistake. I'll have to have a word with that young kitten."

Charlie said nothing.

They hurried to Kit Kat's Café for Fat Alphie's chocolate cake and found Kit just closing up for the night.

"Oh, there you are, Fat Alphie," she said. "I didn't expect to see you. Your young friend, Stanley, said you wouldn't be coming tonight, so I gave him the chocolate cake for your pudding instead. Sorry."

"But not as sorry as he'll be when I get hold of him," muttered Fat Alphie, and his tummy rumbled dangerously.

"But he's just a kitten," said
Charlie the Wimp.

Fat Alphie's
tummy rumbled
loudly in
reply.

Fat Alphie marched back to number three
Wheelie Bin Avenue and found Stanley
asleep in his favourite chair.

Stanley's tummy was nearly as fat as Fat Alphie's.

Fat Alphie poked Stanley's tummy and woke him up.

"I've had enough of you and your tricks," said Fat Alphie. "First you pinch my starter, then my main course and finally my pudding. No friend of mine behaves like that. So pack up your belongings and leave. Right now."

"Ssssorry, Fat Alphie,"
muttered Stanley. "I didn't
mean to upset you."

He hung his head,
slowly packed up his
squeaky mice, his bits
of string and his half-chewed slippers and
headed out into the night.
Charlie the Wimp
watched him go.

"Should you have done that, Fat Alphie?" he said. "He's only a little kitten, and it looks like rain."

But Fat Alphie's tummy was rumbling too loudly for him to hear.

 Chapter Three

Later that night while Fat Alphie
and Charlie the Wimp were tucked up
cosy and warm, there was a big storm.
The wind howled. The rain lashed.
The thunder roared.

"I can't get to sleep for the noise, Fat Alphie," said Charlie the Wimp, clutching his rubber duck and his jingly ball. "Tell me a story."

"Okay," sighed Fat Alphie. "Once upon a time there were two cats, one orange and white cat and one black and white cat.

"One day a little kitten came to stay with the two cats, but he was a real pest, and the orange and white cat got so fed up with him, he threw him out.

"Then there was a storm, and the orange and white cat wished he hadn't thrown out the little kitten… Charlie! Charlie! Wake up. We must go out and look for Stanley!"

"Whaaaaat!" cried Charlie the Wimp.
"Go out in that storm?"

"Yes, we must find Stanley. Come on,
Charlie, out into the rain. You go first."

Fat Alphie and Charlie the Wimp searched everywhere for Stanley. They searched under bushes, but he wasn't there.

They searched under hedges, but he wasn't there either.

Fat Alphie even
sent Charlie to look
up in a big tree, but
there was no sign
of the little kitten.

"He'll be drowned
in a ditch somewhere,"
wailed Fat Alphie.
"And it's all your fault,
Charlie. You didn't
want him to stay."

"My fault," squeaked
Charlie the Wimp.
"It wasn't me who
threw him out."

But Fat Alphie
was too upset
to speak.

Fat tears mingled with the rain on his face
as he trailed back to number three
Wheelie Bin Avenue.

"What shall we do, Charlie?" moaned Fat Alphie. "What shall we do about poor Stanley?"

"Nothing," said Charlie the Wimp. "Look. While we've been out getting soaked he's been safe and warm and dry in our bed. And he's got my rubber duck and my jingly ball."

"Oh, kittens!" laughed Fat Alphie, drying his tears. "What would you do with them?"

Early next morning, before Stanley was awake, Fat Alphie and Charlie the Wimp got busy with a hammer and nails.

"What's all the noise about?" asked Millie the Mouser, strolling past.

"They're making a terrible racket," said One-eared Tom.

"They're certainly making something," said Clever Claws.

Fat Alphie and Charlie the Wimp stopped hammering and banging and showed what they had made.

"Looks like a little house," said Millie the Mouser.

"With a green roof," said One-eared Tom.

"It's emerald, actually," said Clever Claws.

"Wow," squeaked Stanley, bouncing up to join them. "Whose house is that?"

"It's yours," said Fat Alphie.

"We made it for you," said Charlie the Wimp.

"Wow! My very own pad! Thanks, guys,"
said Stanley, and he tried it out for size.
It fitted perfectly.

Fat Alphie and Charlie the Wimp helped
Stanley move in his squeaky mice, his bits
of string and his half-chewed slippers.

Then they went next door and settled down to have a quiet snooze. Number three Wheelie Bin Avenue was peaceful again at last.